F O R W A R D

It's amazing...you slave away at the drawing table, and when you look up next, a fourth book is just completing. Time really does fly!

Between the release of the last book and this one, much has happened in my life: I traveled 700 miles from Idaho to California behind the wheel of a 24-foot long moving truck monstrosity; walked through the revolving door of a brief relationship; I celebrated my birthday in San Francisco, which I haven't visited in 30 yrs.; experienced the painful health scare that is called the shingles; and finally, I was re-united with my family, clearly the best thing out of this whole mess. It was as if someone up there was trying to test my endurance!

Anyway, back to the book. While putting it together, I had the pleasure of revisiting cartoons I hadn't seen in quite some time. This one explores everything, from the possibility of "one trick ponies" to the silliness of "dog marathons". Newbies such as the "jukebox", "store", and "western song" series join the continuing "movie marquee" and "broadway" series, to name a few.

But why am I holding you back? Flip through these kooky pages and experience *Left Field* for yourself!
Enjoy!

the
COSMIC
CARTOON
COLLECTION

by RANDY HALFORD

authorHOUSE®

AuthorHouse™
1663 Liberty Drive
Bloomington, IN 47403
www.authorhouse.com
Phone: 1-800-839-8640

Published by AuthorHouse   06/29/2012

ISBN: 978-1-4772-3731-1 (sc)
ISBN: 978-1-4772-3730-4 (e)

Library of Congress Control Number: 2012911830

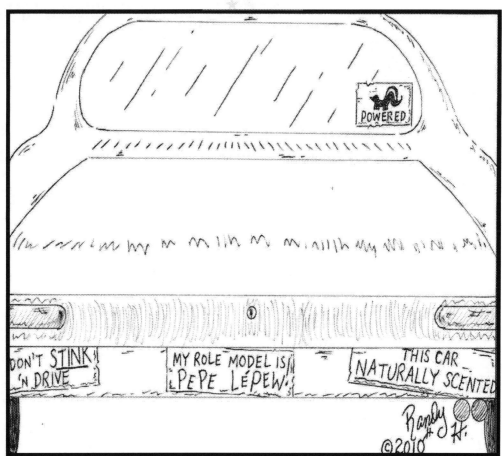

SKUNK BUMPER STICKERS

BEAR FLICKS

"BEFORE THIS GOES ANY FURTHER, FRAN, I'D LIKE YOU
TO SEE THE REAL ME--WARTS AND ALL..."

JOHNNY CARSON IN HEAVEN

"THE EXORCIST: THE MUSICAL"

CAT SCANS

"YOU THE DAWG!"

BILL HANNA'S BACKYARD

MOMENTS BEFORE HIS UNTIMELY DEMISE, DR. VAN HELSING
KNEW HIS POOR EYESIGHT HAD DONE HIM IN: INSTEAD OF "THE
VAMPIRE KILLER'S HANDBOOK," HE CONSULTED HIS WIFE'S COOKBOOK...

THE HEAVY METAL OLYMPICS

"...AND SO, I'LL WRAP UP THIS SEMINAR WITH SOME WORDS OF WISDOM FROM MR. EARL B. HIND HIMSELF: 'WHEN DOING BUSINESS, NEVER LOOK FOOLISH...'"

HIPPIE TELEVISION

DISNEY'S "LADY AND THE TRAMP, PART 2"

THE -LY FAMILY

21

The MATTEL MOVIE PALACE

now playing:
"BARB & KEN & TED & ALICE"

coming soon:

"FULL PLASTIC JACKET"   "VALLEY of the YOU-KNOW-WHATS"
"ROSEMARY'S BARBIE"   "THE BIG BIRD LEBOWSKI"
"GUYS and...WELL...YOU KNOW..." "CABBAGE PATCH ADAMS"
"THE SEDUCTION of G.I. JOE   "HELLO RAG DOLLY!"
   TYNAN"   "PRIVATE DOLL PARTS"
"THE LAST ACTION FIGURE"   "JACK the TEDDY BEAR"
"ST. TICKLE-ME-ELMO'S FIRE"

©2010

DOLL FLICKS

ELTON JOHN'S LULLABY

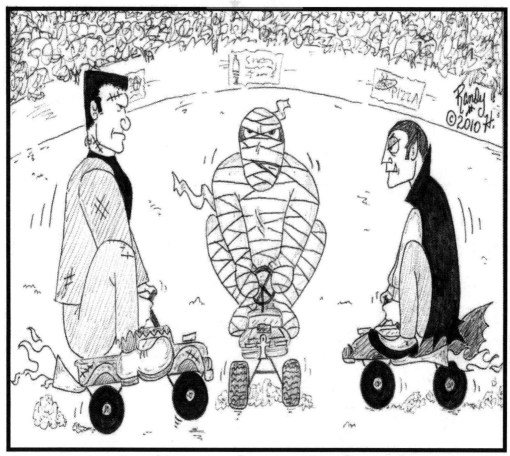

THE PLAYSKOOL MONSTER TRUCK RALLY

HAM RADIO

COMEDY BY NUMBERS

MR. PEANUT'S SUDDEN DEMISE

RING CHIMES OF THE INFAMOUS

"...AND AS I PREPARED TO DEEP FRY THE PARTS (COATED IN THEIR DELICIOUS ELEVEN HERBS AND SPICES)... THERE APPEARED, PALE AND GHASTLY -- WAS A FLOATING CHICKEN HEAD! ITS FACE TWISTED IN ANGER, IT CROAKED OTHERWORDLY: 'WHERE'S THE REST OF ME?!!'"

SCENE FROM "GOODWILL HUNTING"

THE REPETITIVENESS OF PARROT PHONE CALLS

SARCASM UNDER THE SEA

WALT DISNEY: PRIVATE EYE

Ranly
©2010 76

ODE TO TURTLE WAX

OH, YE SPLENDID TURTLE WAX,
HOW YOU MAKE MY CAR EXTERIOR GLOW,
TO THINK YOU WERE NAMED AFTER A CREATURE
SO BLASÉ AND SLOW.
YOU TEMPT ME LIKE A COMFORTING FOOD,
YOUR TEXTURE GOOEY AND SLICK,
BUT TO SAMPLE YOUR SHINY BRILLIANCE
WOULD ONLY MAKE ME SICK.
OTHERS DO NOT UNDERSTAND YOUR JOYS,
THEY CAN ONLY SCOFF.
BUT I PRAISE YOU, SWEET TURTLE WAX,
WITH THE PHRASE FROM "KARATE KID":
"WAX ON! WAX OFF!"

WAXING POETIC

ARMADILLO DATES

WILE E. COYOTE GOES SKYDIVING

MARY POPPIN' FRESH

THE ODD COUPLE OF EGGS

CHICAGO DEEP DISH PIZZA

WAITING TABLES FOR GODOT

©2010

HUNGRY BROADWAY, PART 2

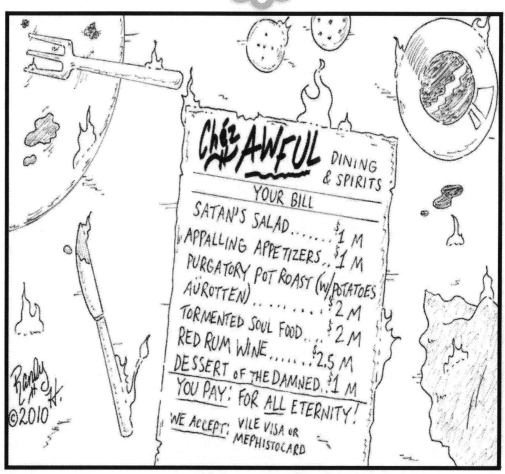

HELL TO PAY

47

MARIO BROS.: ASSEMBLY LINE WORKERS

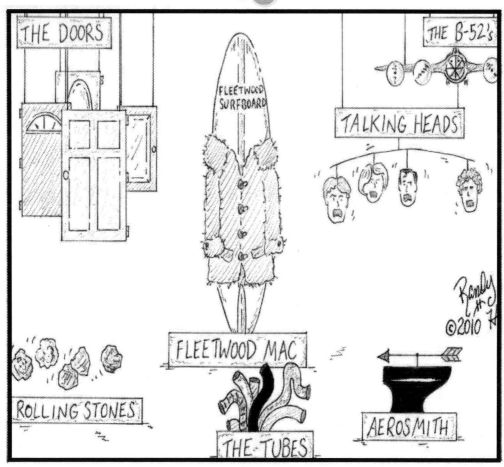

THE MUSEUM of ROCK 'N ROLL ABSTRACT ART

THE LaBREA TAR & NICOTINE PITS

LAUREL & HARDY IN "ANOTHER FINE TOXIC MESS"

MOVIE 639 PALACE

- now playing:

"PEST SIDE STORY"

coming soon:

"THE AFRICAN QUEEN BEE"
"CHARLEY'S ANT"
"ALL THE PRAYING MANTIS' MEN"
"PICNIC"
"THE WEEVIL DEAD"
"BETSY'S WEBBING"
"THE DAY THE EARTHWORMS
STOOD STILL"
"THE LADYBUG KILLERS"
"THE GNAT IN THE HAT"

Randy H.
©2010

INSECT MOVIES

55

ATTENTION DEFICIT DISORDER GAME SHOWS

RIP TAYLOR: GRIEF COUNSELOR

PIRATE RADIO

THE PETRIFIED FOREST

BATHROOM HUMOR

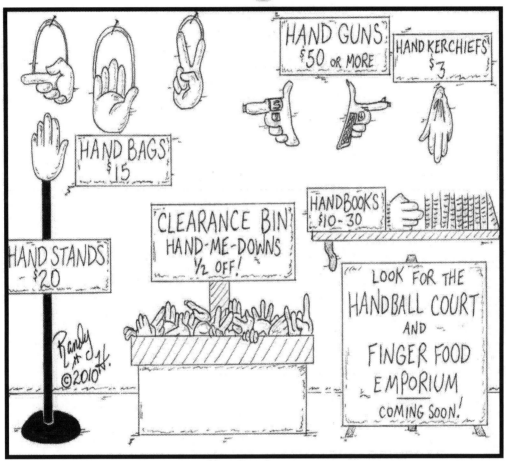

THE HAND STORE

HORSE PLAY

THE MARX BROTHERS IN "A DAY AT THE WHITE HOUSE"

66

The MOVIEQUARIUM

now playing:

"THE CODFATHER"

coming soon:

"THE OUTLAW JOSEY WHALES"
"GORKY SHARK"
"THE SEA HORSE WHISPERER"
"HUCKLEBERRY FIN"
"THE TROUBLE WITH ANGEL FISH"
"THE FLAMINGO SQUID"
"THE GUPPETS TAKE MANHATTAN"
"THE SCARLET SHRIMPERNEL"
"BYE BYE BARRACUDA"
"THE EEL-LUSIONIST"
"VILLAGE OF THE CLAMMED"

Randy H.
©2010

UNDERSEA FLICKS

SNAKE TANTRUMS

YOGA BEAR

THE ROLLING HEADSTONES
BAT BENATAR
DIANA ROSS AND THE SUPREME EVIL
FRANKENSTEIN GOES TO HOLLYWOOD
DIONNE WARWICKED
DEAD ZEPPELIN
HORRID LEWIS AND THE BLOODY NEWS
PETER, POLTERGEIST AND MARY
TONY ORLANDO AND DAWN OF THE DEAD
MALICE COOPER
BILLY GHOUL
THE GRUESOME DEAD
THE HOMICIDAL POLICE
STEPPEN-WEREWOLF
VAMPIRE HALEN
VINCE GUILLOTINE

© 2010

GHOUL JUKE BOXES

THE METAPHOR FAMILY

Sustenance THEATRE

now playing: "HAM-LET"

coming soon:

"LETTUCE of ARABIA"
"THE PAPER CHEESE"
"NIGHT of the LIVING BREAD"
"FONDUE with DICK and JANE"
"THE SANDWICHES of EASTWICK"
"RAGING BOLOGNA"
"MYSTIC PAN PIZZA"
"CHERRY CHERRY BON BON"
"AVATART"
"GOODBYE MR. POTATO CHIPS"

watch for the JAMES BOND festival:

"DR. NO-ONIONS"
"FROM RUSSIAN DRESSING WITH LOVE"
"COLESLAWFINGER"
"YOU ONLY BRUNCH TWICE"
"LIVER LET DIE"
"THE PIE WHO LOVED ME"
"SPOONRAKER"
"LICENSE TO GRILL"
"TOMATO NEVER DIES"
"THE WATERMELON IS NOT ENOUGH"
"DINE ANOTHER DAY"
"CASSEROLE ROYALE"

©2010 Randy H.

FOOD FLICKS

LADY GAGA-LOCKS AND THE THREE BEARS

THE FOOT STORE

DOG TELEVISION

78

SCENE FROM "THE POSTMAN ALWAYS RINGS INCESSANTLY"

COW CAR HORNS

Geritol theatre

now playing:

"THE MATRIX RETIRED"

coming soon:

"GRUMPIEST OLD MEN"
"RAIDERS of the LOST ARTHRITIS"
"THE WRINKLED EYES of LAURA MARS"
"CANE MUTINY"
"GERIATRIC MAGUIRE"
"A WALKER in the CLOUDS"
"SLEEPY OLD COOT HOLLOW"
"ENTER the DRAGGIN'"
"THE MAN with ONE ORTHOPEDIC RED SHOE"
"THE MILAGRO BINGO WAR"
"GRANNY TORINO"
"THE TWELVE CHAIRLIFTS"
"CHILDREN of a LESSER MEMORY"
"THE MEDICATED MEN WHO STARE at OLD GOATS"

© 2010 Randy H.

OLD MOVIES

AARDVARK VENDING MACHINES

THE CULT FILM CLASSIC "PLANET OF THE 80's"

INFOMERCIAL OVERLOAD

GHOST DINING

OCTOMOMS

INJURY & ILLNESS TELEVISION

NO MATTER WHAT LIFE THREW AT HIM, NO MATTER HOW BAD, MYRON TOOK COMFORT IN KNOWING HE COULD BLAME IT ALL ON HIS "PERSONAL DEMONS"...

CRUSTACEAN BROADWAY

PAVLOV'S PETS

PACMAN AT HOME

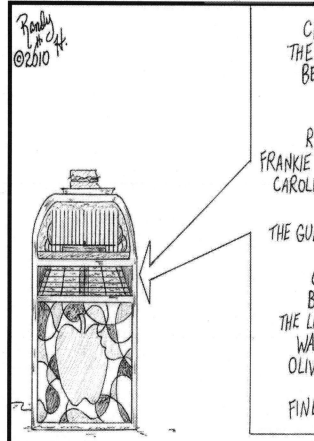

CHUCK BERRY PIE
THE MOODY BLUE CHEESE
BEEF, SWEAT AND TEARS
GRATEFUL BREAD
SOUP-ER TRAMP
RYE AND THE FAMILY STONE
FRANKIE VALLI AND THE FOUR FOOD SEASONS
CAROLE CHICKEN ALA KING
MEAL DIAMOND
THE GUESS WHO'S COMING TO DINNER
RUN DMSEAFOOD
COLLECTIVE SOUL FOOD
BARE NAKED LADLES
THE LOVIN' SPOONFUL OF GUMBO
WANG CHUNG KING NOODLES
OLIVIA FIG NEWTON JOHN
MILLI VANILLA
FINE YOUNG LUNCHABLES

FOOD JUKEBOXES

Randy H.
©2010

MONKEY BUSINESS

THE EAR, NOSE, AND THROAT STORE

WITCH TELEVISION

TROPHY WIVES

DWAYNE "THE ROCK" JOHNSON'S FAMILY PHOTO

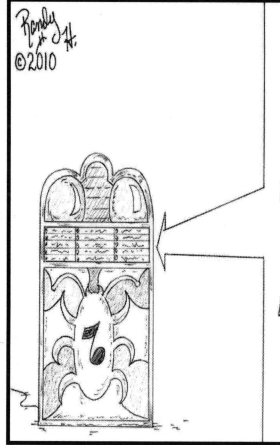

THE DUNG BEATLES
ADAM ANTFARM
BLACK WIDOW SABBATH
BEE BEE KING
THE GRASSHOPPER ROOTS
CATERPILLAR STEVENS
BACHMAN-TARANTULA OVERDRIVE
LADYBUG GAGA
DAVID LEE MOTH
BUZZ SCAGGS
EARTH, WIND & FIRE ANTS
GNAT KING COLE
GLORIA PESTEFAN
QUEEN BEE
NINE INCH SNAILS

BUG JUKE BOXES

SPEEDY ALKA-SELTZER COMMITS SUICIDE

THE BABY MAFIA

FOOD TELEVISION

O'Sacred ✝ THEATRE

now playing:

"MacBETHLEHEM"

coming soon:

"TOP NUN"
"VICAR/VICTORIA"
"PREACH BLANKET BINGO"
"NO COUNTRY for OLD MONKS"
"STAR TREK II: the FAITH of KHAN"
"THE MATRIX ORDAINED"
"GLENGARRY GLEN CROSS"
"PRAY ANYTHING"
"THE CHAPEL SYNDROME"
"THERE'S SOMETHING HOLY ABOUT MARY"
"POPE and GLORY"
"VATICAN of the DOLLS"
"THE BOURNE MOTHER SUPREMACY"
"THE DAYS of WINE and MOSES"
"PULPIT FICTION"

©2010 Randy H.

HOLY MOVIES

THE EYE STORE

ONE TRICK PONIES

FOOD JUKE BOXES, PART 2

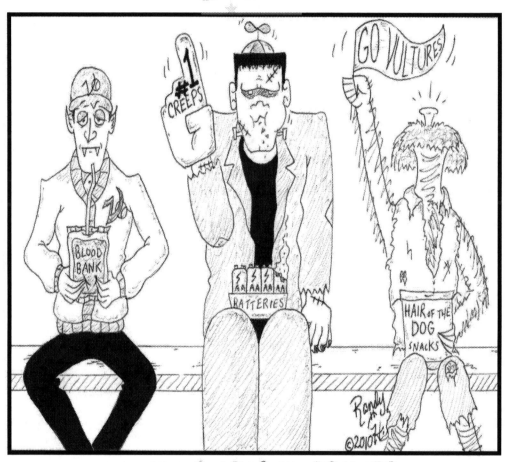

MONSTER SPORTS CROWDS

THE MILITARY DROPS THE F-BOMB

DEEP SEA TELEVISION

OWL SHINDIGS

NOT MANY PEOPLE KNEW DEVIN HAD HIS OWN SELECTION OF "PERSONAL VICES"...

DO-GOODER *theatre*

now playing:

"THE SUPERMAN WHO KNEW TOO MUCH"

coming soon:

"BATMAN of ALCATRAZ"
"KISS of THE SPIDER-MAN"
"WONDER WOMAN of THE YEAR"
"WUTHERING HULK"
"FLASH of THE TITANS"
"CAPTAIN AMERICAN BEAUTY"
"FRIED GREEN LANTERN TOMATOES"
"FANTASTIC FOUR WEDDINGS AND A
FUNERAL"
"DAREDEVIL'S ADVOCATE"
"HUDSON HAWKMAN"
"MIGHTY THOR APHRODITE"
"THE GHOST RIDER AND MRS. MUIR"
"THE MAN WITH X-MEN EYES"

©2010 Randy H.

SUPERHERO FLICKS

DEAD FRED THE ZOMBIE SALESMAN FAILED TO MAKE A SALE.
HOWEVER, HE DID MANAGE TO GET HIS FOOT IN THE DOOR...

THE ACTING BUG

REFRIGERATOR REPAIRMEN FASHION SHOWS

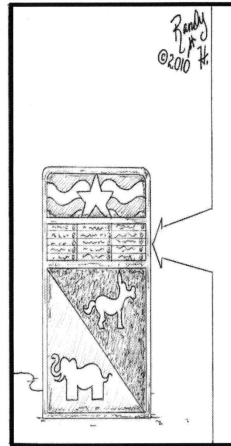

OVAL OFFICE ORBISON
ELECTION JOHN
JFKC AND THE SUNSHINE BAND
THE ALAN PARSONS PRIMARY
KENNEDY LOGGINS
THE ANDREW JACKSON FIVE
DEVO VETO
STEVIE NIXON
KISS-INGER
THOMAS JEFFERSON AIRPLANE
CABINET POST MONKEES
THE FIXX-ED BALLOTS
SENA-TORI AMOS
WHITESNAKE HOUSE
THE STRAY GOV FATCATS

Randy H.
©2010

POLITICAL JUKEBOXES

HELL'S KITCHEN

VEGETABLE TABLOIDS

MIGHTY THOR, GOD OF THUNDERBIRDS

5:00	MANTIS FROM U.N.C.L.E.	6:00	KNIGHT SPIDER	7:00
6:00	COACH ROACH	6:30	WBUG IN CINCINNATI	7:00
7:00	60 MAGGOTS	8:00	DESPERATE HOUSEWORMS	
6:00	FLY WINGS	6:30	BIG BUG THEORY	7:00	NEW
9:00	MOSQUITO TYLER MOORE	9:30	BENNY ANTHILL	
8:00	PEST WING	9:00	ALLY McBEETLE	10:00	NEW
7:00	KING of QUEEN BEES	7:30	EVERYBODY BUGS RAYMOND	
8:00	MOVIE: "SATURDAY GNAT FEVER"	10:00	

INSECT TELEVISION

WONDER WOMAN'S HANG GLIDER

RAT PACK BROADWAY

136

THE CHARLIE CALLAS SPELLING BEE

POETIC JUSTICE

HOROSCOPE SINGLES BARS

SCENE FROM "BACK to the FUTURE 4: DEATH HITCHES A RIDE"

The *Buffet* PLEX

now playing:
"THE LORD of the ONION RINGS"

coming soon:

"FIVE EASY PIZZAS"
"CASSEROLE-BLANCA"
"HAMBURGER HELPER HILL"
"PIE HARD"
"BLUEBERRY VELVET"
"M.A.S.H. POTATOES"
"CAESAR SALAD and CLEOPATRA"
"BEAUTY and the FEAST"
"PHEASANTVILLE"
"JELL-O DOLLY"
"SOUP-ERMAN"
"THE WALNUTTY PROFESSOR"
"THE CURIOUS CASE of BENJAMIN BUTTER"
"THE SUGAR CANE MUTINY"

©2010 Rawley H.

FOOD FLICKS, PART 2

144

OWL-VIS PRESLEY
BOBCAT DYLAN
JOE COCKER SPANIEL
THE SEA MONKEES
CHIHUAHUA - CAGO
PONY BENNETT
BAY KITTY ROLLERS
ANDREW GOLDFISH
THREE FROG NIGHT
LORETTA LIZARD
GERBIL RAFFERTY
TURTLE TRENT D'ARBY
CANARY AGUILERA
STONE TEMPLE PARROT
BILLY GOAT IDOL

PET JUKE BOXES

DR. JEKYLL'S DOG

"IT'S COME TO MY ATTENTION THAT A STAFF MEMBER HAS BEEN PILFERING OUR BEST COFFEE! WHO IS IT? COME NOW, STEP FORWARD...!"

149

JOKE SCHOOL

5:00	I LOVE LLAMA	5:30	DANIEL BABOON	6:00	CHIMPS	7:
6:00	LEOPARDY!	6:30	SEAL of FORTUNE	7:00	STARGOAT SG-1	8
7:00	MARY TYLER BOAR	7:30	WHOSE LION IS IT ANYWAY?		
8:00	MAGNUM PEACOCK I.	9:00	ELEPHANT BONES	10:00	N
7:00	GOAT WHISPERER	8:00	OSTRICH WINFREY	9:00	TM ZEBRA
6:00	CAMEL BURNETT	6:30	PIG BANG THEORY	7:00	E. AARDVARK
10:30	JIMMY CAMEL	11:30	JIMMY FALCON	11:35	CRAB FERGUSON
8:00	MOVIE: "FERRET BUELLER'S DAY OFF"	10:00	NEWS		

ANIMAL TELEVISION

GREASE MONKEYS

Renby
©2010 H.

HERMAN'S HERMIT CRABS
JOAN COLLIE
SIAMESE & GARFUNKEL
BUNNY RAITT
HAMSTER LEWIS AND THE NEWS
TOMCAT PETTY
GOPHER LIGHTFOOT
JERMAINE SHEPHERD JACKSON
DEERS FOR FEARS
LIZARD MINELLI

THE MACAWS AND THE PAPAS
PET TOAD THE WET SPROCKET
HALL & GOATS
PAUL REVERE AND THE REPTILES
PAULA ABDUCK

PET JUKEBOXES, PART 2

NOSTRADAMUS: RESTAURATEUR

DARTH VADER IN A MOMENT OF SELF-LOATHING

DOG GAME SHOWS

Relax Mon theatre

now playing:

"SKA WARS"

coming soon:

"THE EVIL DREAD"
"BANG THE STEEL DRUM SLOWLY"
"LOGAN'S RUM"
"NATIONAL LAMPOON'S JAMAICAN
  VACATION"
"PIRATES OF THE CARIBBEAN BEAT"
"DIVINE SECRETS OF THE YA-MON
  SISTERHOOD"
"CHEECH & CHONG'S STILL SMOKIN'
  DOPE"
"DREADLOCK, STOCK AND TWO SMOKING
  BARRELS"
"REGGAE 'ROUND THE FLAG, BOYS!"
"I LOVE YOU, MON"

"BOB MARLEY & CAROL & TED & ALICE"

©2010 Randy H.

JAMAICAN MOVIES

TURRETS SYNDROME STRIKES SPORTS CROWDS

THE REAL EASTER ISLAND

163

SCENE FROM "PSYCHO: THE VEGETARIAN EDITION"

DOG MARATHONS

THERE WAS A REASON WHY FRANK WAS CALLED THE "HEAD" CHEF...

THE "ROARING" 20's

169

CHARLES MANSON ON "THE SCOOBY-DOO MOVIES"

BRIDEZILLA

SNAKE TELEVISION

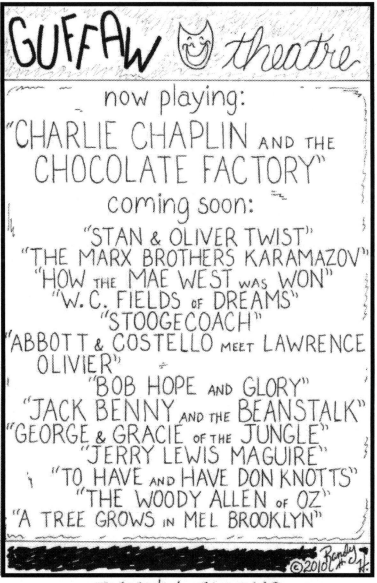

GUFFAW theatre

now playing:
"CHARLIE CHAPLIN AND THE CHOCOLATE FACTORY"
coming soon:
"STAN & OLIVER TWIST"
"THE MARX BROTHERS KARAMAZOV"
"HOW THE MAE WEST WAS WON"
"W.C. FIELDS OF DREAMS"
"STOOGECOACH"
"ABBOTT & COSTELLO MEET LAWRENCE OLIVIER"
"BOB HOPE AND GLORY"
"JACK BENNY AND THE BEANSTALK"
"GEORGE & GRACIE OF THE JUNGLE"
"JERRY LEWIS MAGUIRE"
"TO HAVE AND HAVE DON KNOTTS"
"THE WOODY ALLEN OF OZ"
"A TREE GROWS IN MEL BROOKLYN"

©2010 Bardy H.

FUNNY FLICKS

177

"JUST WHAT WE NEED--ANOTHER 'PYRAMID' SCHEME!"

KILLER BROADWAY

AUTHOR

Celebrating my birthday in San Francisco, 2011

After three books and twenty years in Idaho, author/cartoonist Randy Halford moved back to his native state of California to be re-united with his family. He currently resides in Lodi.

LOOK FOR THESE OTHER LeFT FieLD TITLES...

Which Way to LeFT FieLD™ ?

LeFT FieLD™, RELOADED

LeFT FieLD™ STRIKES BACK!

www·amazon·com